The Calamity *of* Never

YUVIKA
CHAMARIA

BlueRose ONE.com
Stories Matter
NewDelhi • London

BLUEROSE PUBLISHERS
India | U.K.

BlueRose ONE.com
Stories Matter
NewDelhi • London

For permissions requests or inquiries regarding this publication, please contact:

BLUEROSE PUBLISHERS
www.BlueRoseONE.com
info@bluerosepublishers.com
+91 8882 898 898
+4407342408967

ISBN: 978-93-7310-045-6

Cover design: Yash Singhal
Typesetting: Namrata Saini

First Edition: October 2025

Dedication

To those who love like sunsets; softly, fully,
and with no promise of return.

Acknowledgement

This book has taken countless sleepless nights, anxious days, and fragile moments of confidence. There were times I nearly gave up just like when you run toward the high jump, only to freeze right before the leap but somehow, through it all, I had people who helped me gather the courage to take that leap of faith.

To my first and foremost, **Devika Chamaria Harlalka,** my sister by birth but my anchor by choice. It doesn't matter if the world turns its back on me because I know you'll be standing beside me, no questions asked. I don't just love you for being the best sister I could ask for, I love you because you gave me the kind of extended family I didn't know I needed.

To **Aditya Harlalka**, my jiju and also my best friend. Thank you for being my quiet strength, for shielding me from di's drama (you know what I mean), and for always being in my corner. I truly mean it when I say that I love you.

To **Nitya Harlalka**, my little one, small in size, mighty in love. You've shown me what it means to give without expectation. You've taught me more about unconditional love than any life lesson could. I love you endlessly.

To **Neha Chamaria and Niraj Chamaria**, my parents, whose rebellious daughters compelled them to stay ahead of their time and just so you know, you didn't just raise daughters, you raised revolution. You stood by us when it would've been easier to follow the rules, and for that, I carry immense love and respect for you.

Thank you for believing in me especially on the days I couldn't believe in myself.

To **Priyanka Chamaria Agarwal**, my Kuku Di, I know I gave you a tough time growing up (I truly do) but somehow, through all those fights, you became one of the most inevitable parts of my life. Thank you for listening to every poem I nervously read out, and for giving me the kind of feedback that helped me grow every single time.

To **Divyanshi Sarawgi, Pari Agarwal and Shristi Goenka, Vaishnavi Kankani and Yashvi Jain,** my constants, my chaos, my comfort. Thank you for loving me on the days I was hard to love, for listening through the breakdowns, and for reminding me that I could still do this. Sometimes I look at you all and wonder, how did I get this lucky?

To **Evara**, my first book, you were the push I didn't know I needed. You gave me confidence, purpose, and a reason to try again. If you hadn't existed, neither would this one. This book may be new, but because of you, it didn't feel like the first time and that made all the difference.

I am deeply grateful to **BlueRose Publishers** for their faith in my manuscript and for guiding me with such dedication throughout this journey. Their expertise and encouragement have not only shaped this book but also made the entire process a truly memorable and fulfilling experience.

To everyone who picks up **The Calamity of Never,** this may not be the most extraordinary book you've ever read but it holds every piece of me and for you to choose to spend your time with it, I'm more grateful than you'll ever know.

Lastly, to those who stood by me during the making of this book even if your name isn't written here, your presence hasn't gone unnoticed. Thank you for showing up when it mattered the most.

Preface

Some calamities don't arrive with grand warnings.

They don't crash like storms or scream like sirens,

Instead, they whisper.

They slip into your days quietly through a missed call, an unspoken word, a birthday without a voice you longed to hear. They live in paused conversations, silent departures, and the memories that return uninvited at 2 a.m.

The Calamity of Never is not about destruction it's the slow undoing that follows. It's what lingers when something ends without really ending. It is about the kind of pain that doesn't seek to be loud, but still demands to be felt.

There are feelings that don't fit neatly into conversations, but spill easily into poems. Some truths feel safer behind metaphors. This book does not discard these feelings rather empowers you to feel the same.

Each piece in this book carries a fragment of the unspoken; a letter never sent, a goodbye that still hangs in the air. These are the moments we often move past on the outside, but carry quietly for years on the inside. You might find grief here, but also the softness of people who stayed. You might find silence, but if you listen closely, there's also the pulse of survival.

This is not a guide to healing. I don't know if healing always looks like sunlight and closure. Sometimes it looks like making your bed after days of not, or texting someone even when you're afraid they won't reply. Sometimes it's choosing to stay, one more time, in a world that feels too loud for your quiet heart.

I wrote these words during moments I didn't think I'd make it through and somehow, putting them down helped me stay a little longer.

If you're holding this book now, thank you for choosing to listen to the silence between the lines. I hope something here reflects a part of you you've never been able to explain and if not, I still hope it keeps you company, the way certain books once kept me alive.

The Calamity of Never doesn't ask you to be okay. It only asks you to be honest with your heart, with your hurt, with yourself.

Contents

A Museum that Remembered

Room by room,
from the parts of me,
I left unfinished.
Unrequited feelings and
in words that could have been.

No one guards the entrance,
not anymore.
It opens when I flinch,
leading to a massive door,
closes when I am gentle still.

I walk past my own voice,
pressed flat between glass.
Labelled with years,
supposedly was to be kept in the past.

A hallway lined with phones that never rang.
I picked one up, just for the sound of silence to play.
Instead, it yelled the version of me,
that never knew how to leave.
Everything happened for a reason,
I used to believe.

A forbidden room with a big chandelier
and everything precious yet had no locks.

It once let everyone in,
the ones it loved
but as they stepped in,
they didn't know what they broke.
In the room so bright with life,
all there was left was the light of darkness
with broken glass and torn carpets.

The final room with no titles or warning
just memories I wish I could hide.
A microphone wired to the walls
heard me say facts I wish I could deny.

Suddenly before I could blink,
the museum begins to shake
like a breath finally released.
Dust fell in spirals from the ceiling
frames swung crooked as if remembering.
The air smelled of rain that never came,
all I could think was to escape
not only because it could take me in
but also, because I couldn't see it collapse.

Now when I flinch,
I see the final goodbye,
able to let things go.
Learning how to speak
without hiding the echo.

Seven Minutes

Seven minutes, all that she had
before she takes the final goodbye.
People say you see the best memories
in these seven minutes,
moments you lived rewind
just before you die.

She thought to see you,
the one she loved with her
broken pieces
and there was this one piece,
she was scared to lose.

"Not all thoughts are true",
was her last thought before
those minutes were to begin,
before the plucking of the last string.

Subconsciously stored, "special firsts"
that kept her name best defined.
In fourth grade when in a dance competition,
she won the first prize.
Trip to the mountains where she saw her first sunrise,
her first majestic birthday surprise.
One day when she looked at the mirror
and fell in love for the first time.

She once called her best friend two at night
and talked till morning, not realising,
"That's how fast time flies".

She thought to see memories
that were deadly in disguise
instead, God made her see those that kept her alive.

Supporting role?

I like the person standing in the corner,
the one who is supposed to make
the protagonist believe
the world revolves around them.

Amongst the constellations, one star is the brightest,
not because its shine burns through the dark film
but because the rest are dim.

That is why the protagonist exists.
Imagine,
being the reason,
someone is who they are today, Isn't it powerful?
and no one can really take that power away
because not merely needed,
those characters are longed for.

Imagine someone watching
though the person doesn't show up much,
doesn't have many dialogues.
The importance without monologues,
the presence without a face,
the imprint without the appearance.

When the "main character" is less thought about...
if the protagonist is the rain,
the one "tagged along" is the cloud.

Contrastingly, in the eyes of the audience,
the lead is praised
and the one in the corner is merely glanced at
because the centre gets the glory
and the rest are viewed for
being a side character in their own story.

Tower of Cards

Once I was seen glaring upon a tower made of cards,
one that is as fragile as glass.
If lost balance
doesn't take a second to fall apart.
As if it was made to fall
deliberately.
No sooner you realise,
it's too late to do damage control,
so, you let it stay there scattered lonely,
lost what made it "pretty."
People say making a tower of cards
teaches you resilience,
patience to sit for hours,
only for it to fall.
People forget, that
the falling tower teaches you
the "domino effect",
there's nothing left to be built.
Moment of silence before realising,
there's nothing to appreciate
even after the times you spent.
I was caught looking at the tower of cards
but when people thought,
I looked at the building,
I actually looked at it disintegrating
because it tells you the reality behind

the things that scatter need time
to go back to being fine.
The intense glare made them ask what is this about,
to which I said, "definitely not about a tower of cards."

When Time Waited

Some dates stick to your skin
like old perfume or
words you had to keep within.
They hold a history,
not the kind in books
but the kind that sits inside you.

This date reminds me of you
and maybe it always will.
In bits, in pieces,
the kind that leaves an impact,
the kind that is always found in traces.

Without you time didn't really pass
it just stood there
and with every minute
days became difficult to bear.
Ironically you leaving
taught me how to wait,
that clocks break but life doesn't.
It keeps moving yet its steady,
pulling me by the hand
even when I'm not ready.

Somehow,
despite the hollow,
along the softest people
you compensated for your loss
by gifting me the ones who held me,
when I forgot how.

I don't know if healing
ever feels like that fairytale,
rather it was me simply being here.
Trying to catch the clock
despite living in the fear,
what if I never get there?

The clock that once seemed
further apart as seconds pass.
Seems something that can be held
with time and resilience,
maybe I move ahead of the clock itself.

So maybe dates are not just markers,
not endings or beginnings alone
but reminders that even in silence,
we carry what shaped us, what's gone, what's grown
and though the clock keeps moving forward,
I remain caught between then and now
learning that some memories stay,
not to be healed, but to be carried somehow.

Monopoly

Life sometimes feels like a board game
without me knowing the rules.
I move through the haze,
each step steeped in doubt
only so that I could sabotage my 'best move'.
I put on a show to survive another round
hoping next to not be a mere fluke.
When I look around,
I don't see tension, struggle on the 'poker' face,
instead, an evil smirk, 'I exactly know what to do'
masked with a confusing grace.
I can't give up, right?
quitting halfway will only make me a lone outcast
amongst the whimsically competitive players,
they aren't.
Ironically, by just not winning,
I am a loser amongst the losers.
I keep going and anxiously wait for my turn
so, I try and observe, but everyone's so smart,
I almost have no time to learn.
As the clock ticks in a fraction of seconds,
comes my turn.
I close my eyes and play with luck in a game of brains,
the only thing I can count on in this charade.
What if even your last hope turns back on you?
with this, I play my very own calculated move.

"Just another round", in my mind, after all
I guess luck is really not on my side
because while everyone goes for the win,
I simply play to fit in.

After the Applause

I was once told about the effect,
void after good things end,
ones that made you feel alive
are no longer there.

Simply waiting for that one song to begin,
every heartbeat seems rhythmic,
the air hums, making you think if this lasts
you'll never need another thing.

Your favourite series
pulling you to midnight
it's the last episode of the ensemble,
you'd watch it for the last time?

Finding forever in a person,
time bent softer in their presence,
sombre nights turned sweet and long
as if with them, I belonged.

The party begins, lights blurred,
the music so loud,
it didn't let me think
time fades in ways,
I wish it always would.

But change has always been constant
and forever was never that strong.
The rhythm slipped without warning,
what felt endless didn't last long.

The song fades, like it was never sung,
the series ends, its threads all undone.
The party slows, nothing left to say,
the person feels forever, then drifts away.

Voices are now just memory,
rooms emptied silently,
nothing really moves
except the ticking of the clock.

I now understood the meaning,
an abyss, where the fall begins
with no ground below,
an endless void and down I go.

Oasis in a Desert

Summoned to the ground,
tears gushing down her face,
not merely drenched
was swayed along a tidal wave.
She once loved the rains
but don't the loved ones betray?
because its absence caused a heavy drought,
a beautiful forest that once lived inside her
looked like a desert with not a single water spout.
In the scorching light,
a sky so bright,
all she hoped for was clouds,
unlike water, hope never dies out.
The tears she shed during the crisis
became her only hope
as she began to build an oasis.
She could have used it
when she fell and got hurt
to cleanse the wounds left in the dirt,
all she wanted was an oasis to her desert.
Sometimes what you truly want can camouflage
because what could have been an oasis was a mirage.
What she saw was all she needed
but nothing was more imaginative
than its existence.

Silence rewrites memory

Romantic Epiphany

It was not fireworks, storms or lightning,
not sparkles but silence unsettling.
Unaccompanied by grand gestures or a bold sign,
simply came with a moment, I could call mine.

Well love was something I didn't plan,
I didn't count on flower petals in my hand
neither whispered wishes over birthday flames
nor waited for fate to play its game.

I thought love was a puzzle meant to be solved,
a mistook chance or something too far to chase
but rather it walked slowly as if it had to settle
without disguise, without haste.

It was not a question waiting to be answered
nor a sum to be proved.
Just a steady, comforting tailored truth
as if it was only meant for you.

It did not arrive to sweep me away,
but to sit beside me at the end of a day.
A warmth in the silence, a hand in the dark,
not fire, but a slow and certain spark.

Love was never meant to be loud or yelled,
it was the rigid boundaries turning faint,
the line gently bent.
It was not a grand declaration,
rather it was the noise going still.
No thunder, no cosmic decree
just the silence rewriting memory.

Only when love was ought to be a
fairy tale left incomplete,
it instead seemed to turn into something concrete.
What once seemed too fragile to hold, too easy to leave
now became a story the heart could believe.

Perhaps love was never a conquest to win
but a gentle unveiling of where I begin.
Not a finish line crossed to a marathon
nor a prize to attain
but the quiet assurance that nothing's the same.

Romantic epiphanies are strange how they start,
not to the world but a shift in the heart.
No script, no rehearsal nor a borrowed motif
it's just a truth so simple that it remade belief.

Rewind love?

Love is like old hard drives,
filled with thousands of pictures,
fragments of times
you don't even fully remember,
yet they stay engraved,
you tend to love them
even if everything's changed.

The picture you saw
isn't how you'd click a picture now
but you keep looking at it anyway
as if staring long enough
could make you go back.
Wishing for a turn about
on this forward marathon track.

It's like watching an old movie
on a rainy night,
the plot already lived.
A said tale
still carrying its warmth.

There's love, heartbreak,
laughter echoing in dim-lit rooms,
little moments you ache to relive
but can only hold in pixels and memory.

And maybe that's what love really is,
not just what's happening now
but everything that once was.
Everything you keep in the archives,
the moments you return to quietly.
A place where the heart still believes
and all you ever wanted was for it to replay.

Detours

This time it was supposed to be different, right?
but what's different is the time,
your convenience and my ability to bear.
The same thing over and over again
bringing my life to a complete circle.
One which is so frustrating,
exhausting, never-ending.
Making me feel as if the finish sign is missing
around a round marathon track
or when all doors around a
mystery room's periphery seems to be closed.
To you it's nothing much but just another glitch
but to me it's everything,
a malfunction or a permanent shutdown.
This is why I couldn't tell you that this matters to me
so, I still have to keep that smiling frown,
for you to not know that I have had enough
because how long can you take the wrong turns
just to reach the dead end always and all ways.
"It's different from what had happened",
was this your way to convince?
it's the same thing over and over again.
I finally understood what a one-way street looks like,
it's dull, losing its life with no hope of light.

Although to you it's still a small thing?
it's still little?
but it's me who sits in this darkness, and wonder,
for every time I expect a different ending
why do I get the same middle?

Hope in a Fatigued Room

Hope found me in a worn-out state.
It didn't find itself in me, rather
only traces that once existed.
Strings of hope I had built with
resilience began to lose their strength.
They whispered a soft note when plucked,
once music, now a mess.
It looked at me with disappointment,
the way you're seen after committing a crime.
It said, hysterically,
"Who would have thought strings
so strong could sublime?"
I looked at it and said,
"Are you something superficial?"
or maybe it's you who I can't have
but as people say,
there's always some hope left like a ray of light
falling into a dark room through a tiny crack
and with that sliver, it called and said,
"Some strings are better detached before they snap."

Flick

Here she was engrossed in her favourite film
for the fifth time,
acutely aware as the climax unfolded.
Yet she remained motionless,
seeing herself no less than the protagonist
in that profoundly dramatic movie.
Hidden by the leads herself.
A quoted scene rewound and rewatched,
cliche, one in which, I got the one she thought
but here comes the so needed plot;
forever lasted until the scene was shot.
A monologue then began, "I'll wait, no one just leaves",
words were hopeful until the director called, "Cut…",
now lost in the abyss of uncertainty.
Leaving her in the agony
of unfulfilled expectations of naivety,
disappointed as no one thought,
what about the climax she wished to achieve.

Last Conversation?

Hey, where do you go when you just don't feel yourself?

Here, with you.

Okay, but what if someday I am not there then?
Well, will not say I have not thought about it,
I forget that people last, they do stay but for a while,
It is the life's inevitable reality.
Likewise, there are days when I can't help
but think about losing people in the vicinity.
Before that feeling takes over me,
I convince myself that everything is alright, not really.
I don't let people know about my fear of the "goodbye"
in the intention of not bothering
because fears like these are intimidating.
As a wise person once said,
"The tighter you hold, the more they slip away"
and in order to not do so, I'll let you walk your way.

I get it but you know right you can
come to me with any sort of grief?
even if it's something that would
make me want to leave.

No, I can't because having someone
like this is all that I had ever wished,
so how do I tell you certain things
that might be the deal breaking rift.

Why do you feel that something
can really break this deal,
what is stopping you from having that belief?
even though I have always assured
that you don't have to be alone,
it's you who hide these cracks
as if words could mend what's already broke.
I understand there could be certain
things that could hinder balance
but you can express whatever has happened.
Why can't you just simply choose hope over fear?
because to me the weight of silence feels so severe.
It's better to take harsh words
rather than perceiving silence
and it's even worse when it's you who is silent.
The sound of silence hurts
more than loud noises that echo
it can be your escape mechanism
but you need to understand,
your actions leave me with no choice but to ignore.

So, once you ignore,
I feel it's the beginning of the end,
submitting to this silence,
a loop we couldn't really escape.
With no words comes no outcome
compelling us to forget like this never happened.

Maybe, or we just lose interest,
so what's next?
or rather let's talk about something else.

I'M SORRY
IT'S OKAY.

Are You a Liar?

People ask me how I handle lies so well,
I don't. I just learned to lie myself.
Worse than the ones who slip lies for fun,
worse than the ones who get caught and run.
The only difference is, I don't break,
I don't laugh it off, I don't call it a mistake.

Once someone lied, and I couldn't forget,
their words replayed like an unpaid debt.
It wasn't the act that tore me apart,
it was the ease, the tone, the practiced art.

"It was my mistake," they said with a grin,
as if mistakes erase the weight of sin.
So, I thought, maybe that's the key,
say it enough, it sounds like reality.

But somewhere between truth and disguise,
I forgot the sound of honest replies.
Now every word feels rehearsed, confined,
a half-truth tangled with peace of mind.

So now when I lie, it blends, it stays,
almost believable, most of the days
yet I am not a liar at least not to me
because I dress the lies up as truths they can see.

But here's the cruellest twist of all,
the lies I say doesn't stumble.
It lives, it breathes, it learns to grow,
only if someone's willing to call it so.

Silent Cuts

A broken glass,
shattered pieces everywhere till your eyes can see.
It's looked at only when it screams
but after which it was kept aside.
A falling action it wished it could rewind,
lost on fate,
nowhere to reside.
A museum, it thought but then realised,
a glass not merely fallen apart, rather
it was too broken to be called a "piece" of art.
What's worse than being artistically captured?
simply lying there would make others bleed.
Once, someone got a cut and blamed that glass
as if the wounds it left were
an autograph it meant to scar.
It was misunderstood, left unheard
yet no one asked what broke it first.
Too bad its pieces were too hard to find.
It can camouflage its destruction
like people hide their intentions.
Sooner or later, it knew it was getting wiped off
and was to be thrown to where it truly belonged.

Ends Exist?

Some conversations stay in mind,
remains suppressed as thoughts not thought after a while
but days come when I just want to shout it out.
I take a step forward to tell what it's about
but move three steps back fearing my voice to be too loud.
Closer to the end weaker I get,
words untold, unheard,
nothing much to regret?
Well even when I reach the very edge,
I see a path trailing ahead.
The further I reach the further it shifts,
is there really an end?
I think not everything that stops you is from behind,
some are just in front of your eyes
and some unfold with time.
Not everything that's glitter must be divine,
sometimes the shine hurt the eyes,
ignoring the obvious
as if was supposed to make me blind.
With the unseeing eyes,
I overstep on the remains of the blurred line
or was there no line at all,
a step forward is just a softer way to fall.
As one falls from a height,
I wondered where I was amongst the tide?
mind trembles with fright

as the surface is just the beginning
of this sunken sight.
Am I too shallow to deal with depth?
a deeper dive will give me that reality check
so, I sink into it more,
unaware of the depth
and have reached the ocean floor.
Is there a way back?
or to move is to wrestle with resistance,
to fight what one refuses to let go.
It feels like to pull against something
that clings like a shadow.
The force is too less,
my foot was tied to stones
and my hands were too weak to have done it alone.
Exhausted, my breath steadily faints
so, I stay in the self-dug grave.
Where the tide does not crash it's absolving
and I am not drowning I am rather dissolving

Home that Used to Be

Festivals were supposed to be "dancing," right?
but for me, the rhythm cuts short.
It feels like I was built to move
yet left without music
and every silence cuts deeper than sound.

Especially my birthday, I remember.
The first thing in the morning,
I would run and wrap my arms around you,
which was enough to make the day whole.
We would cut the cake,
candles glowing like tiny suns
and when the flame finally surrendered to the dark,
I would close my eyes and whisper
please, never let me celebrate this day without you.

But this year everything is different.
You're not here to be my home.
So, I've decided that,
no noise, no crowd, no celebration
because without you every cheer sounds wrong.
Maybe I don't deserve love on this day,
maybe birthdays are not for me anymore.

The "normal" I knew has shifted
and I'm not ready to pretend.
I don't want tears carving rivers down my face
so, I'd rather stay silent than cut the cake.

Anyways,
what's the point of blowing candles now?
when the only wish I'd make
is the one I already know
can never come true.

I Tried to Pretend

I tried to pretend, as people say.
I tried to pretend I was very happy,
smiling too hard every day
just for you to believe.
I tried to pretend my laughter,
smiling even when I didn't feel like it,
laughing even when I didn't think it was right
so that you don't know it's not been a while
since the last time I cried.
I tried to pretend I was smart enough,
to perfectly portray my emotions to be misleading
because for a fact, I know
you will never resonate with what I have been feeling.
Ironically, I believed I could never be happy anymore
because it's almost every day I used to cry
even while writing this poem
but here am once again laughing
so that you don't know,
I tried to pretend, as people say,
I tried to pretend I was very happy,
smiling too hard every day.

paper is the truth, scissor are words then rock is the heart.

Rock Paper Scissors

Words dig graves no shovel would,
buried deep in the folds of the heart.
They splinter like axes through softened wood,
wounding in places no weapon ever could.

A game I played with innocent hands,
rock breaks scissor, a laugh that descends.
When thought about the cruellest blow
comes from the paper, soft and slow.

Paper wraps rock, just like a lie
gentle enough to justify.
Scissors shred truth in the name of pride
convincing it to seek a corner to hide,
after all the wrong rightly said is right.

Now I realise
words are scissors in silk disguise,
cutting through peace with sharpened lies.
They slice through paper with ease
then flutter like ash in a windless breeze.

I used to laugh at the game we played
but life has rules that never fade
and some of the deepest pain I've known
was carved by lips, not sticks or stone.

So, if I could wish, it wouldn't be flight,
not to soar, nor to shine, nor to set things right.
I'd ask instead for a heart grown cold,
not out of hate, just something bold.

I would wish to have a heart of stone.
A heart of stone, immune to ache,
one no cruel phrase could ever break
but here I stand, still soft, still torn,
by battles of words, not battles of war.

The Midnight Light

One day I look up the ceiling, sleep deprived,
then looked at the clock and it's almost midnight.
I can't sleep at all, my eyes strain,
I just want a break from this insomniac chain.
Nothing puts me off to sleep,
it's all negativity inside,
Then unabashedly my sister switched on the light
even though it's almost midnight.
She came and laid down beside
with a comforting smile that forced me to confide.
Whispered words that worked better than a lullaby,
if you sleep now,
the day you will wake up to is not doomed,
one in which your eyes will meet a healed wound,
experiencing the feeling of having being touched
by a garden of blooming flowers.
Soul not simply bonded by thread
but woven of steel and stars.
Once I was deep asleep, she was teary eyed
and I know she will never tell me why
because when asked she would deny.
The toughest pillar she has been all this while
can't fall weak she thinks.
I wish she would realise,
she built a castle brick by brick
and my dear that's where her story begins.

Invisible?

I once heard someone say they'd wish for invisibility if they had a superpower.
They must be okay with being lost
or with not being found for hours.
A sight never seen, a voice never heard.
That's how you make me feel
because even if you had as many eyes as the stars in the galaxy,
you still wouldn't see the way I see you.
You still wouldn't see what I do.
But I guess that wish will never come true
because even now, you leave me unseen,
ignoring how I might feel.
To you, I'm just someone in between,
just a speck on the screen.
I've shouted. I've screamed
but my voice goes unheard.
So now I stay silent,
though I still have words.
I hide, even when I have reasons to show.
I don't seek company when I'm alone,
maybe I'm just different from before.
So, the next time it's me that you see,
you'll no longer see who you could have seen.

which one would you choose?

A Jar of Candies

Some filled first, to the brim,
some only halfway,
half empty, half full,
depending on who's looking.
I am the kind of jar that shouldn't exist at all,
the one who loves more and is loved less,
who thinks more and is thought about less,
who shows up but is never the one people stay for.
I am the one who takes precautions
but has never been the cure.
A paper that's never a confession,
a brush that never touches the canvas.
In a room of people,
I am still nowhere to be seen.
When choices are laid out,
I am the one left in the shadows,
passed over for someone brighter,
someone easier to love.
Always the friend who watches over,
never the one who's asked, "Are you okay?",
never searched for when lost.
Like a jar shoved to the back of the shelf,
unreached, unnoticed,
because there's always another jar,
brimming with candies,
waiting in the front row.
The one you grab without hesitation.

The one you open instantly,
without ever wondering what waits behind it.
Better, brighter, loved.
And me?
I am still here
half full,
half forgotten.

Transition

I think all I wished was for you to remain the same.
My wish perpetrated,
here you still remain.
The care, the warmth that I thought was forbidden,
you once said thoughts often lie
so, I keep them hidden.
Yet manifest that you still remain the same,
somewhat naive thinking,
time would change my definition of 'same'.
No longer would abide by the promise of
being there during the highs and lows
because the thing about time is
that the truth always shows
yet it didn't show the real you.
Promises still given,
words of affirmations still told,
accurately just how you used to.
Defeating all transitional theories of time itself,
the one who supposedly waits for
none couldn't defy you
so instead it chose to change the person
who you were telling these words to.

Just a Poem?

Words don't easily come to me,
I chase them down reluctantly.
Hours go by for a single line
and even then, it won't feel fine.

The one thing I claimed I knew
slips from my hands and evades me too.
The pen feels heavy, mind in a haze,
lost in an endless, wordless maze.

Pages stare back, a quiet taunt
screaming all the things I want.
The fire that once lit every phrase
now burns in stillness.

Yet still I write, though lines feel late,
not for the crowd, nor to create
but for the self that longs to mend
in broken words that still defend.